Rebel's Tag

K.L. Denman

Orca currents

ORCA BOOK PUBLISHERS

Library and Archives Canada Cataloguing in Publication
Denman, K. L., 1957-

Rebel's tag / written by K.L. Denman.
(Orca currents)

ISBN 978-1-55143-742-2 (bound)
ISBN 978-1-55143-740-8 (pbk.)

I. Title. II. Series.

PS8607.E64R42 2007   jC813'.6   C2007-902772-5

Summary: After receiving a letter from his estranged grandfather, Samuel
begins to learn about forgiveness and knowledge.

First published in the United States, 2007
Library of Congress Control Number: 2007927585

Orca Book Publishers gratefully acknowledges the support for its publishing
programs provided by the following agencies: the Government of Canada
through the Book Publishing Industry Development Program and the
Canada Council for the Arts, and the Province of British Columbia
through the BC Arts Council and the Book Publishing Tax Credit.

Cover design: Teresa Bubela
Cover photography: Andreas Kindler / Getty

Orca Book Publishers
PO Box 5626, Station B
Victoria, BC Canada
V8R 6S4

Orca Book Publishers
PO Box 468
Custer, WA USA
98240-0468

www.orcabook.com
Printed and bound in Canada.
Printed on 100% PCW recycled paper.

010 09 08 07 • 4 3 2 1

For Ron, with love.
KLD

Acknowledgments:
My thanks to those tagged by the moon and ever-deserving of rubies, Shelley Hrdlitschka and Diane Tullson. Thanks also to Tiffany Stark and Jonathan Tweedale for reading the rough cut, and to Melanie Jeffs, Orca Editor, for the fine grit polish.

Author's Note:
Within this story are quotes from writers who set their thoughts on clay tablets four thousand years ago. Those writers were Sumerians and many translations of their ancient cuneiform texts can be found on a website hosted by Oxford University in England at: http://www-etcsl.orient. ox.ac.uk/edition2/etcslbycat.php. I would also like to point out that the characteristics attributed to the planet Uranus in this story are, for the most part, not derived from the science of astronomy. It is true that Uranus takes eighty-four years to orbit our sun, but the notion that planets influence our lives is found in the realm of astrology. It's interesting to note that during the time of the Sumerian civilization, astronomy and astrology were one.

chapter one

I'm late getting home. That sucks because I'll be in for it. Mom hates it when I'm late, especially when I don't have a good reason, like now. I was playing street hockey with the guys and didn't notice the time. No big deal, but I'll hear about how thoughtless I am. How worried she was. How at the very least, I should have called.

I slip into the living room and switch on the TV. Once in a while, if she's on the phone or something, I get away with this ploy. If she isn't sure how long I've been parked on the couch she lets it go.

It doesn't look good today. I've barely landed my butt and Mom's there. I pretend deep interest in the TV, which is useless because I'm watching a diaper commercial. I brace myself for the usual, but she says nothing. Instead she drops an envelope onto my lap. It's one of those big yellow envelopes, and my name is scrawled across the front: *Samuel Connor.* Mom stands over me, her lips pressed tight, her arms folded across her chest.

"What's this?" I ask. "Some garbage from school?"

She shakes her head. "Take a look."

The envelope isn't sealed so whatever it is, I'm betting Mom read it. Judging by the look on her face, she didn't like it. But if it's not a nasty school report, then what else could it be?

Oh, man. Someone must have seen Indi and me doing our thing. They recognized me and reported it to the cops. This envelope is from the cops. They write letters? Wouldn't they just come and hassle me?

I keep cool, reach inside, draw out a sheet of paper. It doesn't have any official emblems. It just looks like a letter, starting with *Dear Samuel*. Weird. No one writes me letters. I shoot another glance at Mom but she hasn't budged. She's just standing there looking like she's going to burst.

I look down and catch an odd aroma wafting from the sheet of paper. What is that smell? It triggers a hazy memory. The memory wheels around the edge of my mind but refuses to solidify. It circles, and I don't want it to come closer. Maybe I don't want to read this letter.

Dear Samuel,

I want to make it clear from the start, us not knowing each other anymore is my fault—not yours, not your mother's. This is your grandfather, Max Connor, writing to you. The last time I saw you was at your father's funeral. You were only four years old, just a little guy. Do you remember me? Because before that day, we were pals and we spent a lot of time together.

I believe I owe you an explanation for being absent from your life. You see, I went kind of crazy after your dad's car accident. Your grandmother Connor died too, just six months before your dad, and I figured I had enough of losing the ones I loved. I decided I wasn't going to love anyone ever again. I made myself forget about you and your mom.

I've written your mom too and told her how sorry I am for being such a fool. If you're reading this now it's because your mom is wiser than I ever was. Ten long years have passed and I've finally got to the place where I know I made a very big mistake. I've asked her to allow me another chance to be part of your life.

I want to give you something, Samuel. It's the most valuable thing I have and I never should have kept it from you. If you're willing to forgive me and accept

*my gift, please follow the instructions
you'll find in the second letter. If you want
nothing to do with a thickheaded old man
like me, well, I understand.*

Your Grandpa Max

The smell coming from the paper is pipe
tobacco. Grandpa Max smoked a pipe.
Two images explode from the past. The
first is Grandpa bending over to scoop me
up, swing me round and set me up on his
big shoulders. The second is him standing
apart from everyone in a graveyard, the
pipe clamped in his mouth. I remember
how I ran to him, expecting to find his
arms reaching down. I caught hold of his
leg and he flinched. He shoved me aside,
sent me sprawling and marched away. I
called after him. He didn't look back.

"Mom?" I say.

"Yes?"

But I don't know what to say next. I
want to crumple that letter, shred it, burn
it. That jerk—who does he think he is? I lift
the paper to my nose and inhale.

"Sam, we need to talk." Mom perches on the couch beside me. She shoves both hands into her hair and scrubs her head, a sure sign she's thinking hard.

"So you read the letter?" I ask.

She nods. She stops scrubbing but keeps holding her head in her hands. "Do you remember him at all?"

I shrug. "Not much."

"We haven't talked about him for a long time. You used to ask for them..." Her voice trails into silence.

Memories of my dad are barely more than those flash images of Grandpa. Maybe I only remember Dad because Mom keeps pictures of him around the house.

Mom straightens, draws in a deep breath, exhales. "I don't know if this is a good idea."

"What do you mean?" I ask.

"Well," she says, "part of me feels sorry for Grandpa Max. But I don't believe we owe him anything. Just thinking about him makes me angry."

"Why?"

"Because of what he did to you," she says. "He knew how much you loved him, and there you were, just a small boy, losing both your heroes at once. I was so shocked at how cruel it was."

Her face is flushed pink and her eyes are shiny. Man I hate it when my mom cries. I tell her, "Don't worry about it. It's history. Who cares?"

"I care!" she says. "It was wrong. You needed him, and he just left you. And now here he is, expecting us to forgive him, like it was nothing."

"So, why don't we just tell him to go to hell?" I ask.

"Sam!" She stares at me for a long moment. Finally she says, "Because I want to be better than that. And I want you to be better than that."

I don't know what she's talking about. I don't want to waste time on stuff like this. I get to my feet and say, "I just remembered, Mom. I promised Indi I'd come over."

"Sam, wait. Maybe we should give him a chance?"

I really want to be out of there so I say, "Sure." Sometimes, that's the only way to stop her: I just agree.

"Okay," she murmurs. Then she reaches into the envelope and pulls out another folded sheet of paper. She looks at it, sighs and then slowly stretches out her arm. "Here. Take it."

I take the paper and stuff it into my pocket. "Catch you later, Mom. I'll be back in time for dinner."

And I'm gone before she can say anymore. There's no way I want anything to do with the old geezer. But then I remember he said he's got something for me. Maybe I should get it and *then* tell him to go to hell. Why not? Seems fair to me.

chapter two

Indi's black brows slant down as she scans Grandpa's second letter. The only sound in her kitchen comes from her long fingers tapping a random beat on the tabletop. Finally she shrugs and sits back. "So, are you going or what?"

"I don't know. I want to find out what the old man has for me, but this seems like a stupid game. Why doesn't he just give it to me?"

"I guess because he doesn't want to," she says. "If it was me, I'd go. What's the big deal? He sends you money and says go to this place and have a burger. Doesn't sound too harsh."

No, it doesn't sound too harsh. Grandpa's second letter was wrapped around a twenty-dollar bill and all it says is that I should go to the Café Soleil on Broadway Street, order a burger and ask for Joe, the cook.

"What if I don't want a burger?" I ask. "I could just take the twenty and get a new CD."

Indi rolls her eyes. "I think you should do what your grandpa asked. If you're nervous or something, I'll go down there with you."

I give her a look. "You think I'm scared?"

She grins. "Aren't you?"

"As if," I say. "Fine. I'll go. Greed wins."

"And you want me to go with you?" Indi's still smiling.

"No, I mean, you can come if you like but it doesn't matter." I really do want her to come with me, but no way am I telling her that.

"Fine," she says. "When should we go? This is sort of cool, isn't it? Like being in a mystery book. What do you think he'll give you? A gold ring? A painting? Or maybe a treasure map! Should we go on Saturday? What if Joe isn't working that day?"

I hold up my hand. "Indi, you're doing it again. Chill."

She giggles. "Sorry. Can't help it."

This has to be the worst part about having a girl for a best friend. She talks too much. Mostly she's fine, but man, there are times when I want to put a sock in her mouth. Okay, so one time I did put a sock in her mouth. It shut her up all right, but then she didn't talk to me for a month. It took some serious sucking up to get her to forgive me. See, that's another thing. You could shove a sock in a guy's mouth and he'd just punch you in the head and that would be it. Simple.

Still, Indi and I have this bond. Probably because we've been neighbors since we were old enough to drool Popsicles on each other. And now, even though she mostly hangs out with her girlfriends and I mostly hang out with the guys, she's the one I go to when I have a problem. Or when I need to go roofing.

"Yeah," I say, "we'll go for the burger on Saturday."

She frowns. "And what if Joe isn't there that day?"

"Then I guess he isn't," I say.

Indi crosses her arms. "Maybe we should call the café and ask."

That's the upside of having a girl around. I wouldn't have thought of that. "Sure. Are you going to call?" I ask.

I get another eye roll as Indi goes for the phone book. She's flipping through it when her father walks in and asks, "Indira, did you finish your homework?"

Indi's dad doesn't say hi to me. He used to like me fine when we were younger. Now? Not much. I think he figures I'm a bad influence on his honor roll daughter. And Indi says her dad is always complaining: "Your friend being a boy is not right." We know what he means, but we laugh about the way he says it. It sounds like being male is a mistake I should fix.

Indi glances up. "Not yet, Dad."

"Well, and when do you intend to do it?" Mr. Bains glares at Indi. "Next year?"

"Dad, I'll do it soon, okay? I just need to make a phone call first."

Mr. Bains mutters something under his breath and stomps away.

Indi makes the call, jots down the address and tells me we'll catch the bus on Saturday at 11:30 AM. "And you're buying me lunch too," she says.

"Anything else, Princess Indira?" I ask.

She sticks her tongue out and says, "Shut up. And go away. I have to do my homework."

I pick up the letter and head for the door but before I get there, I turn back. "Indi?"

She knows what I want, but she shakes her head. "I can't go tonight, Sam. I really have a lot of homework."

"Then maybe I'll go on my own," I say.

Indi plunks her hands on her hips. "You promised me, Sam. Never alone. It's too dangerous."

"What's dangerous?" Mr. Bains is back in the room, his eyes darting between Indi and me.

"Nothing, Dad." Indi's quick answer doesn't cut it with Mr. Bains.

"Nothing?" he asks.

I can lie better than she can. "Indi's just telling me she doesn't want to try rock climbing."

"Hmph," Mr. Bains snorts. "Indira is a smart girl."

I go outside into the dark but don't go straight home. I walk for a bit, my hands in my pockets, my gaze on the ground. I don't allow myself to look up; I have to keep that promise to Indi.

chapter three

"So, what do you think Joe looks like?" Indi asks. We're on the bus, and it's taking forever to go down Broadway. Indi is getting bored and whenever that happens, she starts thinking about what guys look like.

I tell her, "He's probably got rotten teeth, a double chin and wears a long greasy apron."

"Eeuw!" she says. "Nasty. But I don't think so."

"Why not?" I ask.

"Because," she says, "your Grandpa Max wouldn't leave a treasure with someone like that."

"Oh. So you're saying that ugly people can't be trusted?" I ask.

"It's got nothing to do with his looks." Indi lifts her chin and tosses her hair back. "It's the greasy apron I wouldn't trust. Never mind. It's useless talking to you about this stuff."

"Maybe if we talked about good-looking girls instead, I could get into it." I give her my best fake smile.

She elbows me in the ribs. "Forget it. Let's talk about something else. Like, what if you get a ruby ring? Wouldn't that be cool?"

"Yeah," I agree. "Real cool. It might be worth enough to buy a car."

"A car? What would you do with a car?" she asks.

"I'll have my license in a couple of years," I say. "In the meantime, I could work on it."

"You wouldn't really do that, would you?" Indi asks. "Sell your Grandpa's ring to buy a stupid car?"

"For sure I'd do it. I don't need a ring. But a car would be sweet."

"You can be such a loser, Sam." She seems serious.

"Indi, come on. I doubt he's giving me a ruby ring. But if it makes you feel any better and I do get a ring, then..."

"Then you'll keep it?" she asks.

"No, but I could get a ruby red car." I shift sideways to escape the next elbow in the ribs, but she doesn't even try to get me. She just gives me the stare down. Luckily, the bus has finally reached our stop. By the time we get off and find the café, Indi is talking again.

She chatters on about how hungry she is and how good the food smells, and wow, look at all the huge plants. I only half listen because I'm trying to figure out why I feel strange. It's rainy and cool outside, but in here, it's like summer. The café walls are bright gold with streams of yellow paint radiating from a neon sun set high on one wall. Brilliant lights gleam from the ceiling and from lamps on every table. I should have brought sunglasses. I'm standing there blinking when a woman wearing a shiny gold robe walks up.

"Welcome to the sunshine," she says. "A table for two?"

"Uh, yeah. Thanks," I mumble.

The woman leads us to a booth under the neon sun and hands us each a menu. "I'm Goldy, and I'll be your server today. Can I get you a glass of water? Or lemonade?"

"Lemonade, please," Indi answers.

"Sir?" The waitress is looking at me. I don't think anyone has ever called me sir before. This place is quite a trip. Before I can answer, she says, "You look familiar. Have you been here before?"

I shake my head. "Nope. Never."

"Hmm." Goldy studies me for a second more, and then she says, "Well, if you're new, do you know what our café offers?"

"Um," I say. "I think you have burgers, don't you?"

She laughs. "Yes, we do. But we also provide light therapy."

"What do you mean?" Indi asks.

"All of our lighting is full spectrum, which makes it feel like being in the sun. Many of our clients come in on rainy days just to cheer up."

"Oh, yeah," Indi says. "I've heard of that. Some people get depressed when it's gloomy outside, so they use special lights to make them feel better."

Goldy nods. "Exactly. Now I'll get that lemonade for you."

I guess I'm getting lemonade too, whether I like it or not. I flip open the menu but can't focus on it. I'm thinking that Grandpa Max must have come here often and maybe I look like him? Was he depressed? Why else would he hang out in this place?

"I love it here," Indi says. "If the food is good, I'm coming back for sure."

"You're not depressed," I say.

"No, but this really is an upper." She leans toward me and lowers her voice. "So when are you going to ask for Joe?"

I drop my gaze to the menu. "I thought maybe we'd eat first."

"I think you should ask right away," Indi says. "I mean, what if they get really busy? Then he might not have time to talk to you."

As usual, she's right. So when Goldy returns, I ask her if Joe is around. She looks surprised but just asks for my name. When I tell her it's Sam Connor, her mouth rounds into an O and she hurries off again.

"Man," I say, "we didn't even get to order our food."

"She'll be back," Indi says.

chapter four

Goldy doesn't come back. Instead, a huge man emerges from the kitchen and strides toward us wearing a wide smile—complete with teeth. He's carrying something made out of dark wood. When he reaches our table, he sets the wooden thing on the floor and stretches out his hand. I get to my feet before taking his hand. I don't usually have great manners, but there's something about him that makes me stand up.

"Sam Connor!" he booms. "About time we met! Pleased to meet you, boy. I'm Joe." His grip on my hand is crushing. Part of me feels like a weak little kid, but I hold on. I don't even flinch when he releases my hand and slaps me on the shoulder.

"Look at you!" he says. "I can see Max in you, all right." He keeps grinning as he points toward the thing. "For you, from your grandfather. And if I'm not mistaken, you're going to need a burger. One for your friend too?"

"Uh, yeah. Sure. I mean, yes, please. At least, I think so." I'm talking like an idiot.

Indi pipes up, "A burger would be great. Thank you."

"Coming right up. Sam, your grandpa always says the world is a better place when met on a full stomach. Did you know he says that?"

"No, no I didn't," I stammer.

"Well, that's one of his sayings. There's wisdom in that, don't you think?" Joe asks.

"I never thought about it," I say.

"No?" Joe wags a finger at me. "Maybe you should. Max told me he had some poor times as a kid and going hungry made everything harder."

"I didn't know that."

"No? Well, he never talked about it much. He also says there's more than one way of starving to death." Joe gives me a parting pat on the head, and then he's gone. Leaving me with what? I stare at my grandpa's gift and I don't get it. It looks like...

"What a beautiful cradle," Indi coos.

Crap. That's what I thought it looked like. I glare at Indi. "You want it?"

"What?" she asks.

"Do you want it? I don't want it. Talk about retarded. What am I supposed to do with a cradle?"

"I don't know, Sam. But it's not retarded. I'll bet it's an antique. If you don't want it, then you should give it to your mom."

"I don't think my mom plans to have anymore babies."

Indi shrugs. "Then I guess you'll have to wait until you have your own kids."

I just look at her. She looks back, her eyes laughing, her lips smirking. I pretend to scratch my nose, very obviously, with just my middle finger.

That's when Goldy shows up with the burgers. She raises her eyebrows but only says, "Here's your food, kids. And Joe says it's on the house. Cheers."

The burger is excellent, the best I've ever had. Indi and I barely speak while we eat. When we're done, I lean back and sigh. I have to admit, I feel good. Good enough to leave the twenty Grandpa Max gave me on the table, even though I don't have to. I even feel good enough to take the stupid cradle with me. Although by the time I get on the bus with the thing, I'm already wishing I'd left it behind. Everyone who gets on the bus stares at it. A couple of jokers even ask where my baby doll is.

"So lame," I mutter.

"Yeah, they are," Indi says.

I don't bother to tell her I mean the cradle. She knows that's what I meant but she doesn't want to hear me whine about it. She starts telling me about one of her girlfriends who's having problems with her boyfriend. On and on. I don't even bother to remind her she's doing it again. I just say, "uh-huh," sometimes. Mostly I stare out the window and pretend I'm not holding what I'm holding.

There's no way this "gift" changes how I feel about my deadbeat grandfather.

chapter five

Mom's not around when I get home and I'm glad. I ditch the cradle in the kitchen and head out again. With any luck, some of the guys on the next block will be playing street hockey. I'm in the mood to bash something around.

I have no luck. The street is empty. I think about knocking on doors, telling them to get their butts outside. But then I remember Rob had to babysit his little sister today and Jas is grounded. Tim is probably deep into some computer game, and who knows where the rest of them are. It's not worth trying to get anything going now.

Time for Plan B. Whether Indi joins me or not, I'm roofing tonight. I have to. That means I should get a new can of spray paint. I pick up my pace for the walk to the hardware store and think about trying a new color. Red would be good. Ruby red.

When I get home, Mom isn't in the kitchen making dinner. This sucks, because I'm hungry. I find her in the living room, sitting on the floor beside the cradle. She hums to herself and strokes the polished wood as if it's alive.

"Mom?" I say.

She doesn't answer, so I repeat myself. Loudly. "Mom?"

"Hey, Sam," she says softly. Then she sighs. And she starts humming again.

Maybe she's lost it. "What are you doing?" I ask.

Finally she looks at me. "Isn't it beautiful? You slept in this cradle when you were a baby, you know that? And your father too. And his father before him, Grandpa Max."

"Okay," I say. "But why are you petting it?"

She giggles. "I'm not petting it! I was just remembering when you were a baby. You were so gorgeous."

Oh, man. I start backing out of the room. Suddenly Mom bolts up onto her knees, leans over the cradle and stares intensely. Jeez, she really is losing it.

"What's wrong?" I ask. "You see a ghost or something?"

"No," she says, "I just remembered. There's a secret compartment in this cradle."

"What?" In a flash, I'm down on my knees beside her. "Are you sure?"

"Yes," she says slowly, "I'm sure. But I don't recall how it works."

"Well, think, Mom. Think," I urge.

"That's what I'm doing," she says. "Just give me a minute." She starts tapping on the wood with her knuckles. She knocks on the ends, then the sides and finally, the bottom. "There," she says.

"Where?" I ask.

"It's in the bottom. You hear how hollow it sounds?" She knocks on the bottom again.

"Okay, so why don't you open it?" I really want to see what's in that secret compartment. No way would Grandpa Max just give me a cradle. Whatever he wanted to give me must be hidden in there. It could even be a ruby ring, like Indi said.

Mom is muttering. "There's some trick to it. Look at the wood. It's all smooth. There's no handle or anything. Your dad showed me how it works, but I can't remember. I think we have to press somewhere."

"We could break it open," I say.

"Samuel Connor! We cannot break it. How could you say such a thing?"

"Just kidding," I mutter. I wasn't really kidding, but I can see it was one of those things I shouldn't have said out loud. "Maybe you have to turn it upside down?"

"Hmm. Yes, I think that's it." She carefully turns the cradle over and runs her hands over the bottom. When she presses on a spot at the side, there's a soft click and then a section of wood slides to one side.

"Look!" she squeals. Like I might have missed it.

"So what's inside?" I ask.

"Well, it used to have locks of hair," Mom says. "A snip of curl from every baby who ever slept here."

"Nasty! What's the point of that? Collecting DNA for cloning?"

"Oh, for heaven's sake, Sam." Mom slips her hand into the hole and feels around. Sure enough, she pulls out a Baggie holding a hunk of hair. It has a label, *Samuel Connor*. Disgusting. Then she pulls out a few more Baggies. And finally, an envelope. It also has my name written on it.

"For you," Mom says.

Wow. Another freakin' letter.

Dear Samuel,

Do you like the cradle? Bet you think it's an odd gift, but as the first Connor child of your generation, it belongs to you. I was sorting through some things and came across it. Way back when you were around two, you and your folks had to live in a small place for a few months. Your mom asked me to store it for a while, and I forgot to bring it back.

Joe sure makes good burgers, doesn't he? I'm real glad you went and met him. Maybe we'll go down there together sometime? But first, I want to give you something else. I think you'll like this next gift, and hope you don't mind another short trip to pick it up.

Please go to the Dr. Sun Yat Sen Classical Chinese Garden in Vancouver on a Sunday morning. You'll find an elderly man by the ponds, watching the turtles. He'll be wearing glasses and a

31

plaid cap. His name is Henry Chan, and he's expecting you.

One more thing about the cradle. There's a proverb from ancient Sumer, the place some call the cradle of civilization. It goes like this: What comes out from the heart of the tree is known by the heart of the tree.

Your Grandpa Max

I stuff the letter into the pocket of my jeans and go to phone Indi. Mom calls after me, but I ignore her. When Indi answers, I just say, "I'm going tonight, with or without you. I have to."

There's a short silence, and then she says, "Fine. I'll meet you at midnight."

chapter six

The first time Indi and I took a roof, we were eleven years old. We were out playing hide-and-seek one summer evening, and I found a ladder leaning against a neighbor's house. It was too easy. And too perfect. None of the other kids could find us, and we ended up staying on the roof until dark. We got in trouble for staying out so late, and I think that's when Mr. Bains stopped liking me, but it was worth it. We sat there and watched the sky fade from blue and gold to deep indigo. We heard the voices of the other kids drift away. We saw the first stars wink on. And I felt like I was on top of the world.

I remember how Indi and I looked at each other and smiled. It was the sort of smile that said more than words; it said our discovery was incredible and the coolest of secrets. We've been roofing ever since. We've had a couple of close calls. Last fall, a guy heard us on his roof and came outside. He started yelling for whoever was up there to come down or he was going to call the cops. The next thing we heard was, "Blasted raccoons! Go on, get outta here!"

Obviously, he'd spotted a coon and blamed it for the noise. There are lots of them around and they often wander rooftops. Our luck. Another time, Indi slipped on some moss and went sliding. I caught her arm at the same moment her foot jammed into the eaves trough. She didn't go over. That's when she said she'd never go alone and made me promise I wouldn't either. There was one other night when my pants got caught on a tree branch and almost tore right off. That wasn't cool, shuffling home, trying to keep my butt covered.

Other than that, we've got away easy. I don't wear baggy pants to roof anymore, and we decided to only carry stuff that fits into zipped pockets. Plenty of places have a fence, tree or shed close enough to allow us to climb onto the roof. Sometimes we even find ladders lying right alongside the house.

"At least it stopped raining," Indi says when we meet. "Have you already picked a place?"

"I've got a couple of prospects," I tell her. "Let's go."

We walk fast, partly because it's chilly and partly because we're always pumped at this stage. My body feels hyperalive, my muscles are strong, my reactions sharp. I tune into everything around me, pick up on every sound, check out every movement. It's like being in a hunt where we constantly shift roles. We're predators stalking our prey; we're prey on the lookout for predators.

The first house I'd planned to try won't work. The upstairs lights are still on. We go for the next one. It's just a half block farther, and it looks good, all dark. I scoped out the place a couple of weeks ago when I noticed a tall fence running alongside the house. Easy. We lean up against a tree on the street and watch. Listen. All quiet.

"No dog?" Indi whispers.

"I didn't see one earlier. But we'll check." Dogs are a problem. We don't want to find out there's a manic barker after we're on a roof, so we try to avoid them beforehand. We slip into the driveway and head for the front door. The mailbox is our ticket. The tiniest rattle or squeak is all it takes; if a dog starts going bananas, we run for it. Seems like every dog is wired into their mailbox and just lifting the lid gets the dog every time.

I once asked our mailman about this, and he told me postal workers train dogs to bark at them. When I asked why they'd do that, he laughed and said they didn't train dogs on purpose. He explained that dogs figure they're supposed to guard their place. When dogs hear someone at the mailbox, they think it's an attempt to break in. They bark, and right away, the mailman leaves. The dog thinks he scared off the intruder, thinks he did great, and he gets to repeat this almost every day. The mailman said it's called positive reinforcement.

So we rattle the mailbox. Listen. No dog. From here on, we use hand signals. I point to the side fence. Indi grins and points out a flowerpot. It makes a perfect step up, and within seconds, the top of the fence is ours. The roof is right there, an easy scramble. The first part of the roof over the garage is flat. We soft shoe our way across and then pause to study our climb to the peak.

We check for patches of moss and missing shingles. Old wood roofs with missing shingles are the worst because more shingles will break loose under our weight. This roof looks great: it's asphalt, the kind with the best traction. We go for it. My style is to turn my feet sideways, toes pointing out, and just walk up fast. Indi crouches down, uses her hands to steady herself, and goes slow. I always tell her she looks like a monkey, and she tells me to shut up, and there we are, at the top.

I've tried to figure out why being on a roof makes me feel so good. It's as if I've just escaped from suffocating. The air feels free. It even seems I've become part of space, in space. Like I've put my head into the stars. It's weird because I know we're not up very high. It's just that it feels that way, like a different place and time. Indi calls it her *Deva* time—something to do with being among spirits and angels.

We sit and allow whatever it is to soak in. My mind drifts. I let it. And suddenly I'm thinking, there's more than one way of starving to death. I sort of get it. We need more than food to keep us alive. Me, I need to go up on a roof. Nothing else gives me this feeling of freedom. But then I wouldn't die if I stopped, would I? Maybe part of me would die. Is that what Grandpa Max means? I shake my head. I don't want to spend my time up here thinking about him.

What was that other thing he said? *What comes out from the heart of the tree is known by the heart of the tree.* I don't get this. Is he trying to say he knows me? As in, just because I'm from his bloodline or gene pool or whatever, he's part of me. Or I'm part of him?

There's no way he knows me. And I'm done wasting my roof time on him. I reach into my pocket, pull out my spray bomb of ruby red paint and start shaking it.

chapter seven

"Sam!" Indi hisses. "Don't!"

She doesn't like what I've added to roofing. I explained why I do it, but she doesn't get it. It's like this: When we leave the roof, I'll hold onto the feeling for a while. It will last until I fall asleep tonight, but by morning, it'll be gone. And I hate that. I needed to find a way to keep the feeling, and figured it would stay with me longer if I left something up there. I'd be able to think about that thing of mine on the roof, and it would be a link to the magic.

It made sense, but I couldn't figure out what to leave. Everything I thought of, like a feather or a note stuck under a shingle, seemed lame. Plus they wouldn't last. Then one day this girl at school, Molly, told me that my astrology sign is Aquarius. She added, "And your ruler is Uranus."

Man. A bunch of the guys were around and they cracked up. "Whoo. Sam is ruled by his anus!" Molly got all red in the face and tried tell them she meant the planet Uranus rules the sign of Aquarius, but they just howled more. Not that I could blame them.

She started blurting out all this zodiac stuff. "Uranus is a powerful planet, you idiots. It creates radical change. It's behind every rebel..."

She didn't get any further. "It's behind, all right!" someone hooted. At that point, Molly might as well have been trying to talk to a pack of baboons and she knew it. She stomped away. The thing that stuck with me was that Uranus is connected to rebels—exactly what I was looking for. I went on the net, found the symbol for Uranus, so that's my tag. It's easy enough to draw—just the letter *H* with a circle hanging down from the cross bar.

"Make it small!" Indi says.

"Yeah, yeah," I mutter. I do make them small. My little Uranus symbols are on quite a few roofs now, and I'll bet none of the owners have even noticed. I mean, who looks on their roof? Even if they saw something, they'd probably just think it was a leaf or whatever. And until tonight, I've always used black paint.

I have this skitter of nerves just as I press the button on the can. I don't know if it's me or if the can is faulty, but nothing comes out. Then a huge gob of paint bursts from the nozzle and spatters all over the place.

"Omigod!" Indi's eyes are bugging out.

Paint starts running down the roof, and I swipe at it with my hands. This is really dumb because now I have paint all over my hands too.

"You're such an idiot," Indi tells me. Like I don't know.

"Do you have a tissue or anything?" I ask.

Indi starts feeling around in her jacket pocket, and I stare at the mess. It wouldn't be so bad if it wasn't red. Indi hasn't noticed that yet since color doesn't exist without light; there's only black and white and shades of gray. This is going to be bloody obvious when the sun comes up. Yeah, bloody. It will look horrible, like something got killed on the roof.

Indi hands me a tissue and says, "We should go."

I nod. We shuffle down and when we hit the ground, I smell pipe tobacco. I stop dead and look around, straining to hear footsteps, breathing, something.

"What are you doing now?" Indi asks.

"Do you smell that?"

She frowns. "What?"

"Smoke."

"I don't smell anything, Sam. Except paint." She starts walking.

We walk the rest of the way home in silence. When we get there, Indi only says, "I don't want to do this anymore."

I don't argue with her. It wasn't fun tonight. I take one more look around on the street before I go in, but the street is cold and empty.

Sunday morning there's red paint on my pants, so I stuff them in a garbage bag. If Mom asks where they are, I'll tell her I lost them at school; I forgot them in the gym and somebody swiped them. This sucks because they were the best roofing pants I had. I could keep them hidden to wear only when I go roofing. I look at the pants, wadded up in the bag, and know for sure I never want to see those stains again.

I start cleaning my room, throwing more stuff into the bag. It's partly to hide the pants and partly because for some weird reason, I actually feel like having a clean room. I just hope Mom doesn't come by and pretend she's fainting at the sight. For a different weird reason, that would make me feel like messing it up again. Luckily, she doesn't show.

The last thing I toss into the garbage is the letter from the cradle. It's a no-brainer that I'm not going to some dumb garden to meet an old guy. Except maybe I should go, just to send a message back to Grandpa Max. Yeah. I can write letters too. I can write, "Get lost, jerk."

But it's already almost noon, too late for this Sunday. I take the letter out of the bag and throw it on my bed. I can figure this out later. Right now, I need some air. I tell Mom I'm going for a bike ride and head out. I slow down when I get to the house.

An old couple is standing in the driveway, pointing at their roof. I notice stuff I never noticed before, like how the yard is so tidy. The house is clean white. The pale, gray roof looks brand-new. The red paint...it's really red. Some of it's still stuck under my fingernails.

chapter eight

Indi says she's busy, all week. Every time I call, she's out with girlfriends, or doing homework, or something. Finally I go to her house and get her to come to the door so I can show her the letter from the cradle. I wasn't going to tell her about it because I figured she'd try to talk me into going to the garden. Now I'm willing to be lectured just so things can be okay with us again.

I'm wrong.

Indi reads the letter and hands it back to me without a word.

"So," I say. "What do you think?"

She shrugs. "What am I supposed to think?"

"I don't know. Something."

She looks at me. "Sam, it doesn't matter what I think. It's not like you care. Do what you want." And she starts closing the door.

"Indi! Come on. Of course I care. You're my best friend. Aren't you?"

"What's that supposed to mean?" she asks.

I don't know what to say, but I have to say something. I go with, "Huh?"

She does an eye roll. "Are you stupid or what?"

"I guess I'm stupid."

"Too right, you're stupid!" she says. "Anyone with half a brain would know they owe me an apology."

"I owe you an apology?"

Now Indi doesn't know what to say.

Or at least I hope that's why she doesn't say anything. She just glares. I think fast. "Kidding! You know I'm sorry."

"Oh really? For what?" I recognize that look on her face. It's the one that says, *Go ahead. Just try it. And it better be good!* Scary.

"For...for messing up the paint."

"Wrong answer!" The door slams shut.

I stand there, staring at the door for a minute. Then I yell, "And I'm sorry for being a guy who doesn't know what you're talking about!"

Mr. Bains opens the door. "Samuel?" he says.

"Yes, Mr. Bains," I say.

"You should go now."

I nod. "Okay."

Then he adds, "And in my opinion, nobody knows what these girls are talking about at times like this. Not even them."

Before the door closes again, I hear Indi shriek, "Dad!"

Mr. Bains can be an all right guy.

There are tall white walls around the Dr. Sun Yat Sen gardens. I pause before going through the gate. I'm still not sure I want to be here, but it seems like the smartest move. I have this bad feeling that if I ignore Grandpa Max's letter it'll keep bugging me. Sometimes it's just easier to deal with things—especially when those things are like slivers festering under your skin.

I walk in and look around. The pond is easy enough to spot; it's right there, shiny in the spring sun. It's only when I walk up to the edge that I notice gravel paths curving off in several directions, winding between flowery shrubs. Quite a few people are wandering around, but I don't see anyone wearing a plaid cap. A tall Chinese pagoda stands on one side of the pond, and opposite that is another wall with a round gate set into a bridge. It looks pretty cool, like something out of a movie.

The first path I try comes to a doorway leading into a little office. I learn they charge a fee to visit that part of the garden, so I turn and head back the other way. I find benches set here and there near the pond, but none of them hold anyone that looks like Henry Chan. Maybe it would be easier to find the turtles? I position myself on a bridge and watch the water. Orange and white fish flash beneath the surface, and a Canada goose cruises by. When I spot a turtle, only the knob of his head sticks out of the water. I keep watching as he glides toward a large flat rock. Two other turtles are already parked on the rock, and the swimmer decides to join them. His neck comes straining out from his shell as he plants two front feet on the rock and starts climbing. You'd think he was taking on a mountain, the way he has to work for that rock. When he finally makes it, I feel like someone should give him a medal. Then I look up and meet the gaze of an old guy wearing large glasses and a plaid cap. Was he sitting right there the whole time?

"Um, excuse me," I say. "Are you Henry Chan?"

He nods. "And you are Samuel Connor."
It isn't a question.

"Yeah, that's me. My grandfather told me to meet you here."

"It's about time you showed up. What took you so long?" he asks.

"Pardon me?"

"Never mind. You are here now. And here, time moves differently. Like a turtle."

I'm not sure what he means. It's true that nothing in the garden is moving very fast, but I didn't come here to talk about that. I just want him to give me whatever he's got. Still, maybe some small talk has to happen first.

"You like turtles?" I ask.

He considers this for quite a while.

Finally he says, "Why do you need to know?"

"Uh. Well. I don't."

"Then why did you ask? Are there not more important things that you wish to discuss?"

This guy is sort of rude. "Like what?"

And he says, "*Wisdom is better than*

rubies. All the things that may be desired can't be compared to it."

My skin prickles with goose bumps. I stare at him, and his dark eyes behind those big glasses stare back. How could he know? He can't know about the ruby ring.

He smiles and adds, "That's one of your grandfather's favorite quotes from the bible. Did you know that?"

"No, no I didn't."

"Hmmm," he says. "What do you know about your grandfather?"

"Not much," I mutter.

"I didn't think so. He regrets that," says Henry. "He used to sit right here on this bench and tell me about you."

"He did?"

"Yes, and he told me he wished he had been wise. And he wished for you to be wise. Do you know the difference between being smart and being wise?"

I shrug.

"Being smart means you have learned some things. Being wise means that you understand what you've learned—and therefore you know you are ignorant."

"What?"

He chuckles. "Never mind. It is merely a thought. Now, here, I have something for you." He sticks his hand into his coat pocket, withdraws it and holds his closed fist out toward me.

I open my hand, and he places a gold pocket watch in my palm. "Max said to tell you how sorry he is that he hasn't given you real time. This is a fine watch he carried, even though it doesn't work."

"It doesn't work?" I press a tiny button on the top of the watch and the cover springs open. The face of the watch looks back at me, and its hands are still. On the other side of the watch, three human faces look back at me: Grandpa Max, Dad and my own.

Henry says, "Your grandfather told me that picture was taken just a week before your father's death."

"First time I've seen it." I stare at the faces. I know them.

Henry gets to his feet and says, "I must go now." Then he reaches into his pocket again and withdraws an envelope. "One thing more. A letter for you."

I don't know why, but I feel different about this letter. Henry is barely out of sight when I sit down on the bench, open the envelope and start reading.

Dear Samuel,

Do you like the watch? It was given to me by my wife, your grandmother Bess Connor, on our wedding day. You'll find a beautiful picture of her underneath the one of us and your dad. I'm sorry it doesn't work. It stopped just after she passed away, and I never had the heart to fix it. Now, it's time it was repaired. Please take it to Eli Jones at his shop, Space and Time, on Robson Street. He already figured out what's wrong with it and I've paid him too, so don't worry about the cost.

I hope it was sunny in the garden today and that you had a good visit with

Henry. He's a great friend. We met right there on that bench by the pond and have spent many hours swapping stories. The first time I visited the garden, I wasn't too happy, but the place gave me some peace. Might be the same for you? It wasn't long after that I took up studying the ancient land of Sumer. I guess I thought the past might give me some answers. Over four thousand years ago, the Sumerians became the first people to write down their thoughts. The interesting part is people haven't changed much in all that time. Here's another quote from them— this one suits my visits to the garden:

I looked into the water. My destiny was drifting past.

Your Grandpa Max

I get up and walk back over to the bridge. I look into the water. I see myself with the soft gold of the watch shining in my hand. I don't know if my destiny is drifting there. I've never thought much about destiny. I'm not even sure what it is. Something to do with the future? Grandpa saw his future drifting past? And he was all alone? I open the watch and turn it so that the photograph is reflected beside my watery image. I feel something on the back of my neck, a soft touch, like a breath. When I turn, no one is there. And I really wish someone was.

chapter nine

The whole way home on the bus, I stare at Grandpa's watch. It's probably worth a lot, maybe enough to buy a car. But it fits in the palm of my hand perfectly, and I know I won't be selling it. I want to show it to Indi, and tell her how I changed my mind. I figure that by telling her, I might even understand why I changed my mind. Maybe the watch is like that bridge at the garden, only this bridge goes from the past to now. Grandpa Max is getting to me. And maybe I want to see him too? But what if he's disappointed in me? He tells his friends about me like I'm someone special, and I'm not. I'm just an average fourteen-year-old kid who isn't really good at anything.

The bus drives past the house with the ruby red paint on the roof, and I look the other way. But it's there. I feel it the way you feel someone's stare from across a crowded room. It makes me feel way less than average, more like a screw up. I don't want to be a screw up. Not for Indi, not for my mom, not even for Grandpa Max. And just like that, I know what I have to do. Tonight. By myself.

It's strange going out for a roof without Indi. I usually feel like I'm just about to open a birthday present, but not this time. There's no vibe of magic in the air; there's just cold darkness. It doesn't matter. I'm doing this so the magic can happen next time, and the time after that. I know for certain that unless I get rid of the bloody mess, make it right, Indi and the magic could be gone for good.

Once again, the house is dark and silent. I don't bother to check for a dog. I just climb straight up the fence. I make my way across the garage roof and up to the peak without pausing. I pull out a spray can of pale gray paint and start looking for the dark splotches of red. I decided this is the best way to fix it. I thought about scrubbing the roof with some kind of cleaner but chances are that wouldn't work. I had a hard enough time just washing the paint off my hands. Then I thought about that stuff that dissolves paint, but what if it ate into the shingles and wrecked them?

The first few spatters are easy enough to spray over, but some of them are far-ther down the roof. I have to slide along on my butt, bracing myself with my feet to get to them. I don't want to miss any. The last one is very close to the edge, and I lie sideways, stretching out my arm to spray. But as I press the button on the can, I lose my grip, and the can shoots free. It rolls, bounces off the gutter and disappears into darkness. The clatter it makes when it hits the pavement below is unbelievable. It sounds like somebody banging a pot with a metal spoon, the way people do at midnight on New Year's Eve. I've got to get out of here. Fast.

I scramble across the roof, not even trying to muffle my steps. My heart is pounding so hard, it seems as loud as the clattering can. I sprint across the garage roof and jump onto the fence. My shin slides and scrapes along the top of the fence, but I get a handhold and keep it just long enough to steady myself. Then I drop to the ground and start running. And I run right into the old man.

He grunts when I hit him and staggers backward. He starts to fall, his eyes wide and frightened. I reach for him, catch his shirt, catch his arm. We teeter for a long slow second and then tip back upright. We stand there, panting, face-to-face.

"You!" he says. His voice is no more than a hoarse whisper. Anger replaces the fear in his eyes. He coughs a bit, and in a stronger voice he calls, "Mary, I've got him. Call the police!"

chapter ten

The old man doesn't have me. I could push past him right now and run. He'd never catch me. But I want to explain. I want to erase everything. "Wait! Look, I'm sorry! Really sorry. I was trying to fix it..."

"You've got no right being on my property. No right! Damn hooligan!" He shakes his head, points a finger at me. "Didn't your father teach you anything?"

I stare at him, at his disgust, and then a terrible thing happens. My eyes start stinging with tears.

A thin voice comes from the direction of the front door. "Norman? Are you all right?"

"Yes, Mary," he says. "I'm fine. Did you call the police?"

"What's that, dear?" she calls back.

"Oh for Pete's sake!" Norman mutters. "That woman can't hear a darn thing. Kid, come with me."

"No."

"Eh?" he says.

"I'm not coming with you. I fixed the mess. And I'm sorry." I take a deep breath. "But if you're calling the cops, I'm out of here."

His bushy eyebrows draw together and he clears his throat. Then he barks, "What's your name young man?"

"Sam."

"Sam who?"

I start to tell him but then stop. Maybe Norman was a cop himself once; he sure seems like someone I'm expected to obey. I mutter, "Never mind."

We look at each other. Me, with my mouth shut tight, and him, with his head tipped to one side. In a quieter voice he says, "Well, Sam Never Mind, maybe I can give you a chance to explain yourself. But I'd like to go inside because I'm freezing my heinie off out here. Think we can talk about it?"

I shrug. "Yeah. I guess."

"Good. Let's go." He turns and walks toward the front door. Part of me still wants to run, but my feet follow him, right through the door, past a startled Mary, straight on into the kitchen.

Mary follows us and without saying a word, she fills a kettle with water. Norman points to a chair. "Have a seat."

I sit on the edge of a chair and wait.

Norman paces back and forth a few times, and then he lowers himself into the chair across from mine. "Give me one good reason why I shouldn't call the police. No, wait. First I want to know what the hell you were doing on my roof. What's the big idea?"

"Magic," I blurt.

Mary almost drops a teacup. "Magic? Some sort of witchcraft on our roof?" She puts a hand over her heart. "That awful red...!"

"No! Not like that. It's red paint. And it was an accident! I didn't mean for it to go all over the place. I had a faulty can and it just sort of spewed." They're staring at me like I'm talking another language, friggin' Sumerian or something.

I look down at the table. I start again, from the beginning. I tell them about Indi and me playing hide-and-seek. I tell them about loving the feeling of being up on a roof. I tell them about wanting to keep that feeling alive and about the symbol for Uranus. The whole time I talk, they stay quiet. I keep wondering why I'm telling them, but since I started, I keep going. Right up until tonight.

When I'm done, Mary sets a cup of tea in front of each of us and sits down.

I sneak a glance at her, and I swear she's almost smiling. Maybe she didn't really hear what I said?

Norman slurps his tea for a minute. Drums his fingers on the table. Finally he says, "Do your parents know about this?"

"No," I say.

"Well, maybe we don't need to involve the police. But your parents have to know. That's a foolish thing, climbing around on roofs in the dark. You and your friend are lucky you haven't been hurt."

"Listen, Mr., um, Norman. I don't want my mom to find out. And I sure don't want to get Indi in trouble."

"That may be," he says. "But I wouldn't feel right about not telling your folks."

"You can't tell my dad," I say.

"Why not?"

"Cuz he's dead."

Mary clicks her tongue and Norman shakes his head. "I'm sorry about that," he says.

He goes quiet again. I take a sip of tea and Mary gets up. She comes back with a plate of cookies. This is too weird. I'm sitting here at one in the morning on a school night, having tea and cookies with this old couple.

Then Mary says, "I used to love sitting on a roof."

Norman gives her a sharp look, and she takes a cookie and munches. She pushes the plate toward me.

"Mary," Norman says.

"Yes, dear?" Mary says.

"Oh, for Pete's sake! Listen here, if we don't call the police and we don't tell his mother, what the heck are we supposed to do? Shoot him?"

Mary glares at Norman. "Honestly!" she huffs. "You know I can't stand it when you talk like an old redneck. Shame on you. You used to like sitting on the roof too!"

"Well that didn't mean I went sneaking around like a thief, lobbing paint on other folks' houses! Sam here needs to learn a lesson." He looks to me for support. "Don't you, Sam?"

Jeez. I don't think these two ever had kids. They don't have a clue. On the other hand, Norman looks pretty mad again. I nod.

"You see that?" Norman thumps his fist on the table. "Even Sam has the sense to know he's an idiot."

The sense to know I'm an idiot? That's hilarious. Man, I wish Indi was here.

"Fine, then. Have it your way. Shoot him." Mary crosses her arms and looks away, like she's done with this.

"Mary," Norman says.

"Yes, dear?" Mary says.

"You're a difficult woman."

"Yes, dear."

I'm starting to get nervous. What if they're really whackos and Norman does pull out a gun? I point my feet toward the door. Norman holds his head in his hands the way Mom does when she's thinking. But who knows what he's thinking about?

Mary looks at me. "You enjoy painting do you, Sam?"

"Um. Yeah. Sure," I say.

She grins. "Then it's all settled. Our shed needs painting something terrible. You can start tomorrow. Mind you now, I don't want red. I want white and gray to match the house."

Norman's head comes up, and then his arms spread wide. "Why didn't I think of that?" he asks.

"You would have, dear," Mary assures him. "You would have. Now, Sam, you'd best run along. Norman will have everything ready for you after school tomorrow. Isn't that right, Norman?"

Norman nods. I go while the going is good.

chapter eleven

All day I feel like that turtle trying to drag its butt up onto the rock. By the time school is out, I'm way too tired to paint a shed. After I got home last night, I barely slept. These questions kept repeating in my brain: Why were Norman and Mary so nice to me? Did they forgive me? How? I'm just some kid they don't even know who messed with them.

I don't think it's that easy, forgiving someone. I think if I go to Norman and

Mary's, I'll find out they're still mad. I really don't want to go there. It's not like I told them I would. They just assumed I'd go along with their plan.

And another thing: Why am I stuck with all these old people lately? What's up with that? Enough already.

So I go home. I need to relax. But I look out the window and see Indi walking down the street. I want to go hang with her, tell her all this stuff. Only she hasn't forgiven me, has she? I don't get it. I make myself a snack, turn on the TV, flip through the channels, and there's no way I feel relaxed. I keep looking at that cradle Mom left in the living room. I keep pulling the watch out of my pocket and looking at it. I feel like crap.

It's no use. I have to go paint the shed. I have to find out how they forgave me. *If* they even did.

When I get there, the first thing I look at is the roof, and it's not good. Norman is up there. He's wobbling around like a kid doing his first roll on a skateboard.

Mary is standing in the driveway yelling at him.

"You're an old fool, Norman. Get down from there!"

He says something back and she says, "What's that, dear?"

He yells something about Pete.

Man.

I shuffle up the driveway and stand beside Mary. "Um. Hey. What's up?"

Mary doesn't miss a beat. "Norman is up. See if you can make him come down, won't you, Sam?"

What can I do? I yell, "Norman?"

He startles and this is bad because the wobble gets worse for a second. Then he straightens up and turns, very slowly, to glare at me. "You missed a spot!"

He's right. I can still see that last splotch of red, down near the edge of the roof. "So let me get it," I say.

He shakes his head. "Too late. I'm already here."

"Oh, my Lord," Mary murmurs. "He is so stubborn."

I see what's going to happen now. He's going to fall. That crazy old man is going to slip and crash and roll off the edge of that roof. He's not going to bounce and clatter like the paint can. He's going to bust all over the pavement like a watermelon...And it's my fault. My fault.

"Please!" I scream. "Stop!"

Norman says, "For Pete's sake! You two are a royal pain in the arse, you know that? A man can't go up on his own roof for five minutes without all this jabber? Fine. I'm coming down."

"Thank goodness," Mary breathes.

"But not until I cover up this spot!" And Norman sinks to his knees, shimmies down the slope, raises my can of gray paint and takes aim. Sprays. Breaks out in a huge grin. "There! You see? I did it."

He did. He got the spot. The ruby red is gone. I raise my fist in the air. "Yeah, Norman! All right."

He's not going to fall. He wobbles across the roof and dangles his feet over the edge to find the rungs of a ladder. I sprint over to hold it for him. When he reaches the ground, he's still grinning. And wobbling. Only the wobble is more like a swagger, like he just scored a major touchdown.

"How about that?" he says.

"Cool," I tell him.

"Darn right. Cool."

"I think we need a cup of tea," Mary says.

"Mary?" says Norman.

"Yes, dear?"

"I don't need a cup of tea. I need a..." He stops.

"Yes, dear?" Mary frowns.

"A cold one, dammit. How about it, Sam? Join me in a soda pop?"

I really thought he was going to say something else. "For sure," I answer. "A pop would be good."

So we have a pop. Nobody mentions the shed until I bring it up. "Um. So, did you get the paint?"

"Eh?" says Norman.

"For the shed," I say.

"Well, now," says Mary. "Norman and I had some words about that. I want the shed painted gray with white trim and he wants white with gray trim. We just don't know. What do you think, Sam?"

I look at them. There is no right answer. I shrug. Then I blurt, "What I really want to know is why you forgave me."

They stare at me like I just spoke friggin' Sumerian again. Finally, Norman says, "Well, you were sorry, weren't you?"

I nod.

"Okay. That's what we thought. And we're too old to stay mad. Not enough time for that," says Norman.

"Huh?"

Mary pats my shoulder. "What he means, dear, is life is too short to waste it holding a grudge. If we stayed angry, why, we'd feel just dreadful. Anger is an awfully heavy thing to carry around. It wears you out something terrible."

"Not only that," Norman says with a wink—an actual wink. "This whole deal gave me a chance to impress my woman here."

Mary giggles.

I can't help it. I say, "You've got to be kidding me."

"Nope," says Norman.

"Well," I say, "okay. Thanks. A lot."

"You're welcome," they say, together.

"Tell you what," I hesitate, and then go ahead. "I'll be happy to paint your shed when you decide about the color."

"We knew we could count on you," Mary says.

"Could be decided when hell freezes over," Norman says.

Mary clucks her tongue. "Such bad language, Norman, with the boy's cabbage ears listening."

They are so weird. Nice. But weird.

"There is one thing though," Norman says.

I feel my shoulders hunch. "Yeah?"

"We'd feel a whole lot better if we knew you weren't going on roofs in the dark anymore. If we thought you were going to keep doing that, we'd have to speak to your mother."

I don't have an answer for him, but I feel something slipping away from me, something I've had since I was eleven years old. I don't want to let it go.

chapter twelve

When I get home, Mom has dinner ready. We're halfway through the meal when she gives me one of her mother looks. "Are you feeling all right, Sam?"

"I'm fine."

She frowns. "You don't look fine."

She tries to put her hand on my forehead, but I shift away. "I'm okay. Just a bit tired."

"Just tired? I wonder. Is something bothering you?"

I shrug. "Nope."

Her gaze narrows. "Is everything all right at school?"

"Yup. All fine."

"What about with you and Indi? She hasn't called lately."

Man, mothers sure can be nosy. "Mom, everything's okay. Indi's just busy right now." I shove in a mouthful of food so she can't expect me to say more. No way can I tell her Indi's mad at me because her questions wouldn't stop and I can't explain. I'd be grounded for life if she knew what happened.

"What about Grandpa Max?" she asks. "Have you heard from him again?"

I don't want to tell her about Grandpa Max either. Not yet. Part of me wants to show her the watch, but then she'd want to talk about that too. Give me advice. The whole deal with him—I want to work it out on my own. I'll show her the watch as soon as I've got things figured out. But she knows I got another letter out of the cradle. I have to tell her something.

"Yeah, Grandpa Max said he forgot to return the cradle. He stored it when we lived in some small place. It's supposed to go to the oldest Connor grandchild."

This is the perfect thing to tell Mom. Her face lights up. "That's right! I'm so glad he remembered to give it to you. It's wonderful to have a family heirloom like that, isn't it?"

"For sure." I yawn. "Man, I'm really tired. Think I'll go do some homework and then go to bed early."

She nods and I make my escape.

I head for my room but can't even think about homework, never mind do it. I think about Indi instead. Maybe I finally know why she's so mad. It's got to do with me taking something away from her and being too stupid to know I was doing it. I work it around and around in my head but can't make it simple. Not simple enough to put into words. I keep trying. I practice mumbling the words. *Indi, I'm sorry I didn't see ... I'm sorry I didn't get how you felt about ...*

I can't picture myself saying this stuff out loud. But maybe I could send her an e-mail? It takes a while to get something that sounds okay:

Hey, Indi. How's it going? Listen, I know why you're mad at me. It's because I wrecked our kid magic. I knew you didn't like me tagging the roofs. It's like I was leaving garbage on a mountain. But I didn't care about what you thought. And when it got ugly, you couldn't stand it anymore, right? So I'm really sorry. I think I know how you feel. The magic is gone for me too. That sucks. I wish some things didn't have to change. Like us being best friends?
Sam

Five minutes later, the phone rings. "Sam?"

I feel a rush of relief. "Hey, Indi."

"I read your letter," she says. "It's good."

"Thanks." I take a deep breath. "I really screwed up, huh?"

There's a pause. Then, "Yeah, you did. You're human. But you know what?"

"What?"

"I was really upset too because the roof magic is history. Only I think it would have happened sooner or later. It's not all your fault. Some things just stop fitting."

"Yeah. I guess." A prickle runs over my scalp. I don't want to be one of the things that doesn't fit.

"Like my dolls and my stuffies. I gave most of them away the other day, and my mom was practically crying."

"No way."

"Way. I think she'd keep me a baby forever if she could. You know my friend, Sarah?"

"Yeah?"

"We were talking about this stuff and we can't wait to finish school. It's going to be great. Her cousin graduated last year, right?"

"Right," I say.

"Now she's gone backpacking in Europe. How cool is that?"

And off she goes, talking a streak. Just like always. I don't tell her to stop. I just soak it up. After a while she asks, "So what's been going on with you, Sam?"

"A bit. I'll tell you tomorrow, okay?" It'll take an hour to tell Indi everything, and I'm too tired to talk anymore.

"Okay. Want to hang out after school?"

"Yeah," I say, "that would be good."

"But, Sam?"

"What?"

"Letting stuff go...like the roofing," she says, "it is sad."

It is. But when we hang out after school and I tell her everything, I feel okay. Like everything's all right. Indi loves my gold watch. She hugs me when I tell her there's no way I'll sell it. She can't wait to meet Norman and Mary. And she totally takes over planning the trip to Space and Time.

"Can I go with you? I'm going with you. Let's go on Saturday. No, wait. Why not tomorrow, after school? Oh,

I can't. My cousins are coming over. But maybe Friday?"

"I don't know. I'm not in any hurry."

"But don't you want to get the watch fixed? Maybe this Eli guy can give you your grandpa's phone number or something. Don't you want to see him?"

Do I want to see him? I still don't know. I need to think about it. I guess I do, but maybe that means I have to forget that he ran out on me. I look at Indi and say, "Yeah, I want to get the watch fixed. But there's no rush. We'll go in a while."

She narrows her eyes and studies me. I put on a smile and shrug.

"Okay," she says. "Whatever. Let me know when you're ready."

It takes a few weeks before I'm ready. I think about it every day. Part of me is itching to see Grandpa Max. But the other part still resents how he ditched me.

I wasn't important enough for him to bother sticking around.

He's a stranger. Is he a stranger?

Terrible feelings come out of the past. Feelings about dark holes and awful losses. There are murky memories of my mom crying at night. Hating the cards we made at school on Father's Day. Quitting soccer because there was no dad, no *man*, to slap my back and say, "Good game!"

I feel ripped off. I don't want to take a chance on him.

And then I re-read his letters. There's that question in the very first one. Am I willing to forgive him? I think about how Indi forgave me. Norman and Mary too. They said there wasn't enough time to hold a grudge. I think about Mom saying she'd rather do better. I think about how losing people he loved made Grandpa Max want to hide. And I get it. He's human. He didn't know where he fit anymore. Maybe, after all this time, he fits with me again?

How can I *not* forgive him? And when I get to that thought, it just happens. And I find out that forgiveness feels like being on a roof. Like freedom.

Space and Time is such a narrow slot among all the shops on Robson Street that we walk past it twice before we find the door. The store is barely wider than the doorway, but once we're inside, it stops being small. The room stretches back, long and narrow. And it soars up, way up, into blackness. There must be a ceiling somewhere, but all I can see is space. Models of every planet in the solar system hang above our heads. Indi and I stand still and crane our necks.

"There's Uranus," I say.

A chuckle emerges from the clutter on our left. "Careful," a voice chides us. "The correct way to say it is YOOR-ah-nus."

"What?"

"You heard me. So, you like the cosmic trickster?"

"The what?" I say.

"Astrologers say Uranus causes all sorts of trouble when it orbits through certain transits."

"Um. Yeah." I look for the owner of the voice and find a grinning young guy wearing a weird pair of glasses. He almost blends in with all the clocks and gizmos. "Are you Eli Jones?" I ask.

"That's me. And you are?"

"Sam Connor. My grandfather..."

Eli cuts me off. "You're Max's grandson." He isn't smiling anymore.

"Yeah," I say. "I've got his pocket watch. He said you could fix it."

"Well, yes. I can." Eli hesitates. "I guess I can understand why you'd want that now."

I don't know why, but I suddenly feel cold. "What do you mean?"

"I mean, considering. You know."

The chill increases. "No, I don't know. What are you talking about?"

Eli looks away. He pulls the glasses off. He steps out from behind the counter and raises his arm, like he's going to hug me. I shrink back, and he lets the arm drop. "Look," he says, "I was really hoping you'd find out some other way. Like maybe someone would tell your mom. I don't know why Max asked me to do it. I'm not really good with words. But Max asked me to tell you. If it happened to play out like this. I couldn't say no."

And I know what he's going to say.

chapter thirteen

My voice seems to come from somewhere outside of me, but I have to speak. "He's dead, isn't he?"

Eli nods.

Indi shuffles up close and puts her arm around me.

"When?" I croak.

"Day before yesterday." Eli clears his throat. "He had cancer. He just couldn't hold out any longer."

I want to hit something. Hit it really, really hard. My hand forms a fist and I pull away from Indi.

"Whoa, there. Easy!" Eli steps toward me again. "I'm sorry, Sam. I wish things had gone differently for you guys." He lifts his hands, palms up. "I'm really sorry."

"Why didn't Henry say anything?" I yell. "He knew Grandpa was dying, didn't he? You knew. Why didn't you tell me? You're supposed to be his friends, aren't you?"

"Yeah. We are. And believe me, we argued with him about it. But he made us promise not to tell. He hoped you'd see him because you wanted to, not because you felt sorry for him."

I pull the watch out of my pocket and drop it on Eli's counter. "That's not good enough. It's not right."

Eli nods. "Maybe so. You think we should have broken our word to him and told you?"

I stare at him.

Eli shakes his head. "He knew you were mad at him when he didn't hear from you. He said he understood that. But now...Well, I hate to come down on you at a time like this, but who are you most angry with now? Him, for taking too long to get over the past? Or yourself, for doing the same thing?"

"Nobody told me there was a time limit!"

"There's always a time limit, Sam. Always."

I can't think of anything to say. We stand in silence, and then I hear them. The ticking of clocks. Lots of clocks. Marking off the seconds, the minutes, the hours. Clocking life. I find myself staring into the face of a tall, wooden clock—a grandfather clock. And the anger drains out of me as fast as it took hold.

I feel that breath again, on the back of my neck, but I don't turn this time. I know he's not there. Not in the way I want him to be. "Come on, Indi," I say. "Let's go."

"What about the watch?" Eli asks.

"Keep it," I say.

"Sam, wait. He wanted you to have it. I'm going to repair it. And I have one more letter for you." Eli dives behind the counter and pulls out a familiar-looking envelope. He holds it toward me. "Please. Take it."

I can't take it. But Indi reaches out and Eli hands it to her. "I'll give it to him later," she murmurs.

"Good. And one more thing. Just so you know. He didn't want a funeral, but he'll be buried on Monday, next to your grandma and your dad."

I start walking. I burst outside and march down the street, my feet pounding the pavement double time.

"Sam!" Indi calls.

I walk faster, harder, my arms pumping at my side.

"Wait up, will you? Sam, please stop."

I don't want to stop. What does she want from me? There's nothing to say. I just want to be alone right now. I need to be alone. Buried next to my Dad? I see that deep, black hole in the ground. My father's grave. Grandpa walking away. I start running. I'm not looking back.

Not looking back.

Not looking.

Not.

Grandpa Max, when he left Dad's grave, and left me...He never looked back.

I stop.

chapter fourteen

Indi is crying when she catches up to me. "I'm sorry, Sam! I'm so sorry."

I just shake my head.

"It's my fault," she sobs.

"What? What are you talking about?" I ask.

"I should have made you come down here sooner. But I let you wait, even though I had this bad feeling...I'm sorry!"

I can't say anything for a minute. My thoughts are spinning. Her fault? "That's crazy, Indi! It's not your fault. I wasn't ready."

She hiccups. "But I should have talked you into coming."

I take hold of her arm and give it a little shake. "Indi, I don't know who to blame, but it's not you."

She sniffles. "But the way you took off from me..."

"It wasn't you," I say.

"Okay." She takes a deep breath. "I know that. But it's not your fault either, Sam."

I take a big breath too. "Does it matter whose fault it is? It doesn't change anything. Maybe this is just the way it had to be. Like destiny."

"Wow." She looks at me like she's never seen me before. Slowly, she adds, "You're way ahead of me, Sam Connor."

"Yeah?" I know what she means. But I don't want to talk anymore, so I come up with a feeble joke. "That's because I run faster."

"Sam. You know...never mind. Let's go home."

And for once in her life, Indi stays quiet. When we get off the bus she gives me a hug; then she puts Grandpa Max's letter in my pocket. "We'll talk later, okay?"

I nod. "Thanks, Indi."

"Hey, anytime."

Her words echo as I go inside and up to my room. Anytime. Anytime.

There's always a time limit.

I think about Norman and Mary saying there's not enough time to stay angry.

There's always a time limit.

I think about Henry Chan saying, "It's about time you showed up."

All those clocks ticking away the time.

I open the letter. The writing looks different.

Dear Samuel,

A kind nurse is writing this for me. Hope you don't mind. The medicine I'm taking makes me clumsy. The next thing I have to tell you is how sorry I am we never got to meet again. The cancer is moving fast now. I thought I had more time. Someone my age ought to know better.

All I can say now is I hope you get to be wiser than I ever was. When you were a wee boy, you were so much like me. Stubborn. Sensitive. Curious. A bit of a rebel. I loved you for it. Seems like some qualities really are bred in the bone. Known by the heart of the tree? But like anything, those things have a good and bad side. The thing to do is build on your good traits. Do you think being stubborn is a bad thing? It sure can be, and I proved it. But the flip side of that is it also gives you the strength to endure. You see?

I was slow in figuring that out. Being sensitive and stubborn, I held a grudge against life itself. It wasn't a wise thing to do. I let you down, and myself too. I missed out on knowing you. The things I really wish I'd given you are love and time. My time. The cradle and the watch are poor substitutes, but it gives me some comfort that you have them.

I don't know if any of this makes sense.

I'm sorry. Nurse says I'm doing fine, and I want to say one more thing. If you ever get a chance, please look at the planet Uranus.

The Nurse is looking at me like I'm crazy. I never did get to see Uranus because it takes so long to make its orbit—eighty-four years. To tell you the truth, I don't know why I'm curious about that planet. Eli Jones says all free spirits like Uranus and it puts its mark on some of us. I'd say the Uranus rebel mark means the need to find your own path, to not accept the ordinary. I wasn't a free spirit, but I wish I had been. I was finally heading that way. Maybe now, when I move on?

Well, dear boy, I'll say farewell. Please know that you come from a cradle of love. Make time for all that's important. Look up to the vast unknown, and dream.

Love
Grandpa Max

chapter fifteen

There aren't many of us gathered at the grave. My mom, Indi, Joe the cook, Henry Chan and Eli Jones. There is no minister. We stand in awkward silence, waiting.

Waiting for what? It's wrong to lay a body in the ground and not say anything. I feel this. I think all of us do. Everyone shifts from one foot to the other. We keep our eyes down. A couple of guys in work clothes stand behind us. Finally they come forward and begin shoveling dirt. It goes over the coffin, covers it, starts filling the hole. We keep waiting.

For what?

At last one of the workers speaks. "We can show you the headstone now. It's ready."

We nod.

And they bring the stone. It doesn't stand upright, like I expected. Instead, it's flat. We all lean forward to read the words written there.

Maximilian Connor
To be alad; such is my hope.

"There's a mistake," I say.

One of the workers pauses, looks at the stone, shakes his head.

"No mistake," Henry says softly.

"But a lad is two words." I point at the stone. "They didn't leave a space."

"You must recall," Henry murmurs, "your grandfather studied the Sumerians."

"Yes?"

"I believe your grandfather sent you one more message. He told me about this word, *alad*. He found it amazing. In English, it suggests a boy. True?"

I nod.

"But in Sumerian, the word means a male protective spirit."

"Ahhh!" My mom breathes. And her eyes fill with tears.

Then Indi starts to cry.

"Too cool," says Eli.

"The man was solid," says Joe.

In a soft voice, my mom says, "I'd like to say something." She pauses, and her gaze settles on a small bird perched in a tree. She nods. "The peace prayer of St. Francis.

"Make me a channel of your peace,
Where there is hatred, let me sow love;
where there is injury, pardon; where there
is doubt, faith; where there is despair, hope;
where there is darkness, light; where there
is sadness, joy.

"O Master, grant that I may not so
much seek to be consoled as to console;

to be understood as to understand; to be loved as to love.

"For it is in giving that we receive; it is in pardoning that we are pardoned; and it is in dying that we are born to eternal life."

We're quiet again. I feel like saying something too, but can't find the right words. I nudge my mom and whisper, "Thanks."

She smiles and hooks her arm through mine. "Ready?"

I nod, and we turn away. The others follow us back to the parking lot and raise hands in farewell. Then Joe calls out, "Listen, I'd sure like it if you all came down to the café sometime."

He's looking at me.

Henry stops and looks at me too. "In case you're still wondering, I do like them."

"Um. What?" I ask.

He busts into the craziest laugh I've ever heard. "Turtles! Come and see. Slow is not always wrong." He's still cackling when he drives away.

Mom stares after him. "Sam?" she asks.

"It's okay, Mom. I think he's just saying he liked Grandpa Max."

The sun does not give up easily. It leaves a ruby red glow on the horizon. The ruby deepens to purple. The sky darkens to indigo and then black. The stars wink on. Some planets are showing up too. I check my pocket watch and can barely read the numbers, but it tells me the time is right.

Even though it's a warm summer evening, Norman and Mary are huddled under a blanket. We're on the flat roof over their garage, and Indi's there too. So is Eli with his telescope.

"Anytime now," Eli says. "It'll be near the constellation Aquarius. Should appear blue-green in color."

He's talking about Uranus. It's supposed to be visible through a telescope tonight.

Even if we don't find it, we know the free spirit is out there. And here too, with all of us.

K.L. Denman was born under the sign of Taurus, which is ruled by the planet Venus. She very much likes the idea that Venus is the planet of harmony and love while also bestowing the tendencies to be creative and enjoy beauty. However, the notion that Venus can also influence one to be materialistic and lazy concerns her; she intends to guard against those traits.